Mole's Useful Day

Tales from Whispery Wood

Make friends with the animals
of Whispery Wood!

Be sure to read:
Flying Friends

... and lots, lots more!

Mole's Useful Day

Julia Jarman
illustrated by Guy Parker-Rees

■SCHOLASTIC

To Sam and Theo – J.J.

Scholastic Children's Books,
Commonwealth House, 1-19 New Oxford Street,
London, WC1A 1NU, UK
a division of Scholastic Ltd
London ~ New York ~ Toronto ~ Sydney ~ Auckland
Mexico City ~ New Delhi ~ Hong Kong

First published by Scholastic Ltd, 2002

Text copyright © Julia Jarman, 2002
Illustrations copyright © Guy Parker-Rees, 2002

ISBN 0 439 99455 1

All rights reserved

Printed and bound by Oriental Press, Dubai, UAE

10 9 8 7 6 5 4 3

The rights of Julia Jarman and Guy Parker-Rees to be identified as the author and
illustrator of this work respectively have been asserted by them in accordance with the
Copyright, Designs and Patents Act, 1988.

Chapter One

It was winter in Whispery Wood. Snow fell silently, piling up beneath the old oak tree. Owl and Bat were sleeping inside the tree. Squirrel was in his drey. Only Rabbit was awake, in the entrance of his burrow.

Suddenly Rabbit jumped
as one of the snow-piles
moved!

Then he saw a big pink snout!
"Wakey, wakey!" shouted Mole.
"Shush," said Rabbit.
"You'll wake
the others."

"That's what I'm trying to do," said Mole, in a loud voice. "Unless you want to play with me?"

Rabbit shook his head. "N-no. N-no thank you, Mole. N-not today." Rabbit looked around anxiously.

Mole was fed up. She had played by herself all morning. Now she wanted someone to play with.

"WAKEY, WAKEY!"
she shouted again.

Then she threw a snowball at Owl.

It missed – luckily.

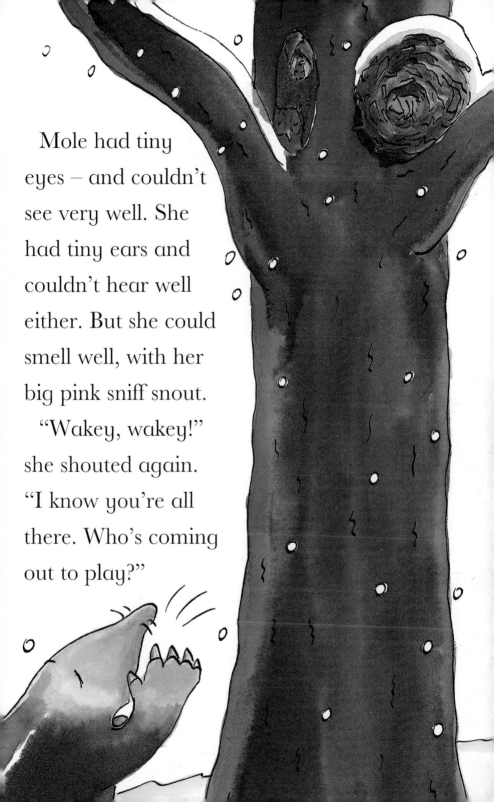

Mole had tiny eyes – and couldn't see very well. She had tiny ears and couldn't hear well either. But she could smell well, with her big pink sniff snout.

"Wakey, wakey!" she shouted again. "I know you're all there. Who's coming out to play?"

"Oh dear," said Rabbit. "Please don't wake Owl. He's been so grumpy since he lost his reading glasses."

But Mole threw another snowball.

It missed again, but Owl hooted crossly.

"Mole, it is three o'clock in the afternoon. You know I sleep during the day. And it's winter, if you haven't noticed. Bat sleeps in the winter. So does Squirrel on bad days. Why don't you play with Rabbit? He's awake."

"Rabbit doesn't want to play," Mole replied. "I don't know what's the matter with him. I've been playing by myself all morning. I've made a snow mole and a snow owl. Look."

"Very nice," said Owl. "Very lifelike."
But Owl had other things on his mind.
He flew down to Rabbit's burrow.

"Why are you sitting outside?" he asked kindly. "It would be much warmer inside your burrow."

Rabbit's teeth were chattering. "I heard some scratching at the b-back of my b-burrow," he said. "I think Weasel is trying to b-break in."

Owl understood at once. Poor Rabbit was too scared to go to sleep.

"If I woke up and found Weasel looking at me, I'd j-just freeze," Rabbit went on. "And then…"

Rabbit stopped, but Owl knew what would happen next. Weasel moved fast and he had very sharp teeth.

"You should have told me earlier," said Owl.

"I d-didn't like to d-disturb you," said Rabbit.

 Chapter Two

Owl quickly took charge. "Right Mole,
it's time to make yourself useful."

"Useful?" said Mole.

"Useful means helpful," said Owl. "And being useful will stop you being bored. First, check the walls of Rabbit's burrow. See if Weasel has been trying to break in. Next…"

But Mole didn't wait to be told what to do next. She dived into Rabbit's burrow.

The walls seemed safe enough, except in Rabbit's bedroom. Weasel had been trying to break in!

Mole set to work with her big shovel paws.
First she mended the wall.
Then she made it thicker, so Weasel couldn't get through.

She liked being useful. Owl was right.
It did stop her feeling bored.

When she had
finished, she
hurried back
to Owl and
Rabbit.

"You were right about Weasel," she said.
"But he can't get in now – not through the
back. I've made the wall thicker. What can
I do now?"

"You can guard
the front," said Owl,
flying back to his hole.
"Rabbit can keep a
look-out. You can keep
a sniff-out. If Weasel
comes back, give me
a shout. Don't try
and tackle him
yourself," Owl
warned. "That
would be
dangerous."

For several minutes, Mole and Rabbit sat outside Rabbit's burrow.

Mole sniffed the air. Rabbit tried to keep a look-out, but his eyes kept closing.

"Why don't you go inside and have a good sleep?" said Mole. "I've made your burrow safe. I can keep guard now."

"Thank you, Mole.
I do feel rather
sleepy." Yawning,
Rabbit went into
his burrow.

Mole went on sniffing – for a while.
She sniffed to the north.

She sniffed
to the south.

She sniffed to the east and west.

Then she started sniffing
all over again, but all
she could smell was
clean, snowy air.
There was no sign
of Weasel at all.

After a bit, her big shovel paws felt itchy.

"Bother, I'm bored again," she said to
herself. "I'll have to think of something
even more useful."

Suddenly, she had a brilliant idea.

She was thinking it through when Robin landed on a low branch.

"Have you seen Weasel?" said Mole.

"I think he's in the meadow, on the other side of the river," said Robin.

"Perfect! Thanks Robin."

Quickly, Mole covered the front of Rabbit's burrow with snow.

Then she wrote
a note to Rabbit.

She pinned it to the oak tree and set off,
heading north.

Dear Rabbit,

Don't worry. You
are quite safe and
I am going to make
you safer. I'm going
to catch Weasel!
Friendly regards,

Mole

At first she travelled over ground. Then
she began to tunnel through the snow.

"What are you doing?" said Robin, flying overhead.

"You'll see in a minute," said Mole. She carried on tunnelling, singing as she went.

"Half a pound of wriggly worms
Half a pound of beetles
Left and right and left again —
Then Plop goes the Weasel!"

"It's a maze!" said Robin. "A snow maze!"

"Exactly," said Mole, pausing for a moment. "I'm going to catch Weasel in it. But I can't stop now. I've got to tunnel my way to Hedgehog's. He's part of my plan."

It didn't take Mole long to reach Hedgehog's house. There he was, fast asleep under a pile of leaves. He had rolled himself into a tight prickly ball and was snoring loudly.

"Wakey, wakey!" shouted Mole. "Don't you want to be useful?"

But Hedgehog just carried on snoring. He was deep in his winter sleep.

Mole backed out of the tunnel. "Never mind. You can still be useful, Hedgehog. When Weasel runs into you he'll get a short sharp shock!"

At last the snow maze was finished. It ended just in front of the bridge.

Mole told Robin her plan.

"Weasel will race over the bridge – plop!
– into my maze. And he'll be trapped.
The sides are so high
and slippery!"

"Hmm," said Robin,
"but why will he race
over the bridge?"

Mole held two long leaves above her
head. "He'll see these and
think I'm Rabbit," she
said confidently.

29

"Hmm," said Robin again, flying off. "It might work. I wish I could stay and watch, but it's past my bedtime."

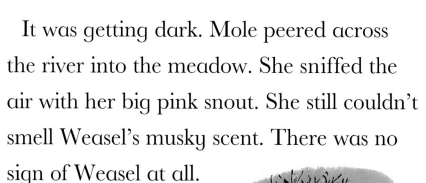

It was getting dark. Mole peered across the river into the meadow. She sniffed the air with her big pink snout. She still couldn't smell Weasel's musky scent. There was no sign of Weasel at all.

But Mole was being tricked by the wind.
It was blowing Weasel's scent away from
her ! Weasel was in fact very close, hiding
behind a hedge,
watching
Mole...

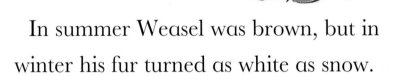

In summer Weasel was brown, but in
winter his fur turned as white as snow.

As he watched, he couldn't believe his luck.
What a tasty first course Mole would make!

The sky grew darker and Weasel began to creep closer.

Chapter Three

Back at the oak tree, Owl had just woken up.

"Rabbit! Mole! Where are you?"

Rabbit came out of his hole as Owl flew
down to investigate.

"I'm here, Owl! Don't worry. I'm all right.
Mole is keeping guard."

"But Mole isn't keeping guard," said Owl.
"Mole isn't here."

"Oh dear," said Rabbit.
"She isn't, is she?
I wonder where
she's gone."

Then Owl noticed the letter pinned to the oak tree.

"Read it to me, please," said Owl. "I'm useless without my reading glasses."

Rabbit read quite slowly.

"Isn't Mole brave?" he said when he'd finished.

"No," said Owl, flying off. "Mole is silly and impetuous – she acts without thinking. I just hope I can find her before Weasel does. Come to the river as fast as you can."

Chapter Four

Back at the bridge, Mole was peering into the meadow. She thought Weasel was still there.

"Half a pound of wriggly worms," she sang at the top of her voice.

"Half a pound of beetles
Try and catch me if you can…"

Then she stopped as a musky
smell reached her snout.
Suddenly, Mole
saw a weaselly face.

She dropped back into the tunnel and ran
as fast as she could.

Weasel dived in after her – causing an
avalanche!

Mole headed
for Hedgehog.

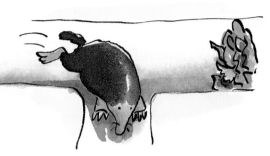

She turned right
just before she
reached him.
Then she quickly
built a low wall
and lay in wait
behind it.

Soon she smelled Weasel. Then she saw
him gliding past – very fast.

Then she heard a loud
"OUCH!" as Weasel ran
straight into Hedgehog.
Mole clapped her
shovel paws. Her
plan was working!

"Easy peasy! That scared Weaselly!"
Laughing, Mole began to dig a tunnel
back to the old oak tree. But there was
something blocking her way.
What was it?

Hesitating for a moment, Mole didn't
hear Weasel coming up behind her. By the
time she smelled him it was too late.

"Pop!" sneered Weasel.

Mole looked round and found herself
staring into Weasel's bulging eyes.

"Oh no,"
she gasped,
as Weasel took
a step towards her...

High in the starry sky, Owl was swooping
and swirling, searching desperately for Mole.
But where was she? And where was Weasel?

Suddenly Owl saw the maze, saw something pink glowing in the moonlight. Could it be Mole's pink sniff snout?

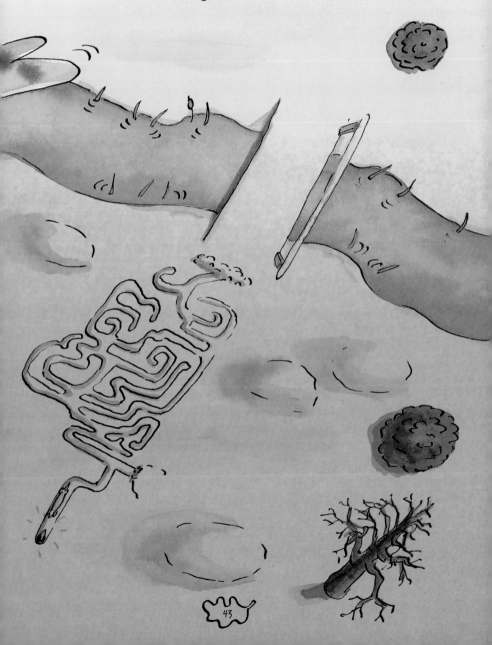

Far, far below, Mole thought her last
moment had come. Weasel was
getting closer, but she
couldn't move.

His bulging eyes stared into hers.
"I am going to eat you.
I am going to eat you.
I am going—"

"For a swim!" said Owl, swooping down, then swirling up with Weasel in his claws!

Mole and Rabbit reached the river just in time to see the...

SPLASH!

Rabbit clapped. "Thank you, Owl. You've taught Weasel a good lesson. He won't come back to Whispery Wood in a hurry."

"I hope somebody else has learned a lesson," said Owl, looking severely at Mole.

"Oh Owl," said Rabbit. "Please don't be cross with Mole. She helped scare Weasel away. She was a *bit* useful."

"No she wasn't," said Owl grumpily. "She wasn't useful at all."

"Oh yes I was," said Mole. "Look what I found in my maze!"

"My glasses!" hooted Owl. "A-mazing!" And the three friends laughed. Then Owl said, "Thank you Mole," and they all raced back to the old oak tree.